Aram's Choice

For Carl Georgian, whose father
was a Georgetown Boy.
M. S.

For my grandson
Jasper Ethan and his father Jonathan Augustus with Love
M. W.

NEW BEGINNINGS

Aram's Choice

By Marsha Forchuk Skrypuch

with illustrations by Muriel Wood

Fitzhenry & Whiteside

Published in Canada by Fitzhenry & Whiteside,
195 Allstate Parkway, Markham, Ontario L3R 4T8

Published in the United States by Fitzhenry & Whiteside,
311 Washington Street, Brighton, Massachusetts 02135

10 9 8 7 6 5 4 3 2

Library and Archives Canada Cataloguing in Publication
Skrypuch, Marsha Forchuk, 1954-
Aram's choice / Marsha Forchuk Skrypuch ; illustrated by Muriel Wood.
ISBN 1-55041-352-X (bound)
ISBN 1-55041-354-6 (pbk.)
1. Armenian massacres survivors—Ontario—Juvenile fiction.
2. Armenian Boys' Farm Home—Juvenile fiction. fiction.
3. Georgetown (Ont.)-Juvenile. I. Wood, Muriel II. Title.
PS8587.K79A73 2006   jC813'.54   C2005-907263-6

U.S. Publisher Cataloging-in-Publication Data
(Library of Congress Standards)

Skrypuch, Marsha Forchuk, 1954-
Aram's choice / Marsha Forchuk Skrypuch ; illustrated by Muriel Wood.
[256] p. : col. ill. ; cm.
Summary: A young orphan and survivor of the Armenian genocide in Turkey is one of fifty boys
chosen to make the long journey to Canada and a new life in Georgetown, Ontario.
Note: Based on the recollections of one of the original Georgetown Boys.
ISBN 1-55041-352-X
ISBN 1-55041-354-6 (pbk.)
1. Armenian massacres survivors—Ontario—Juvenile fiction. 2. Armenian Boys' Farm Home—
Juvenile fiction. 3. Georgetown (Ont.)—Juvenile fiction. I. Wood, Muriel. II. Title.
813.54 dc22   PS8587.K79A73 2006

Fitzhenry & Whiteside acknowledges with thanks the Canada Council for the Arts,
and the Ontario Arts Council for their support of our publishing program. We acknowledge
the financial support of the Government of Canada through the Book Publishing Industry
Development Program (BPIDP) for our publishing activities.

 Canada Council   Conseil des Arts
for the Arts   du Canada

 ONTARIO ARTS COUNCIL
CONSEIL DES ARTS DE L'ONTARIO

Design by Wycliffe Smith

Printed in Hong Kong

Table of Contents

June 10, 1923

On the island of Corfu, Greece

Quickly, boys! Form a line!" called Mrs. Walker.
Aram Davidian looked up from his game of
marbles. Mrs. Walker was standing in front of the
old barracks. The crumbling army building had been con-
verted into a dormitory. He and hundreds of other
orphaned boys lived there.

Sarkis, Mikayel, Zaven, Vartan, and some of the older
boys were playing marbles, too. Most of the other children were swimming in the sea, their bodies glistening in
the sun.

Mrs. Walker put one hand on her hip and used the
other to shade her eyes from the glare. When Aram saw
Mrs. Walker put her whistle to her lips, he stood up. The
whistle shrilled. Instantly the boys stopped splashing, and
swam to shore. Aram and the rest of the boys ran to the
barracks and formed a line.

Aram stood between Mgerdich and Taniel. At twelve,
Aram was one of the oldest boys in the group. And he felt
luckier than most because he had a grandmother who was

still alive. Taniel was lucky, too. He had an older sister at the girls' orphanage. Poor Mgerdich had no family left. Nine-year-old Mgerdich reminded Aram of his own younger brother, who had vanished while they were trying to escape from Turkey.

Mgerdich looked up at Aram with a toothy grin. "Do you think she has a treat for us?" he asked hopefully.

"Maybe," said Aram. Wouldn't it be wonderful if Mrs. Walker pulled out a giant bag of sugar-coated almonds, or maybe oranges? Aram's stomach growled at the idea. The missionaries did a good job of scrounging up food for all their boys, but the menu was limited. Sometimes Aram thought that if he ever saw another bowl of mashed up lima beans, he would vomit.

"Attention," said Mrs. Walker. "There is someone I would like you to meet."

The door of the barracks opened and their sports teacher, Mr. Chechian, stepped out. Many of the teachers at the orphanage were university professors and scholars who had also escaped from Turkey. These men were anxious to teach the boys as much as possible, and sometimes their lessons were boring. Mr. Chechian was different.
He did fun things. He taught them all how to swim like fish, and he took them on long hikes and camping trips.

Following Mr. Chechian was a man the orphans had never seen before.

"Please welcome Mr. Melkonian, children," said Mrs. Walker.

"He is an Armenian shoemaker, and he lives in Canada."

Aram looked at Mgerdich. "I wonder what he will be teaching us?" he whispered. Mgerdich shrugged.

"Some of you will be going to Canada," said Mr. Melkonian.

Aram could feel his heart go flippedy-flop. He had heard about Canada. It was a country so rich that you could pick gold from the trees!

"And I want to tell you about it," continued Mr. Melkonian. He opened his bundle and pulled out a stubby black boot. "Who can tell me what this is?"

Aram put up his hand.

"Yes?"

"It is a soldier's boot."

"Close," said Mr. Melkonian. "This is a Canadian snow boot."

Many hands went up. Mr. Melkonian pointed to a boy at the far end of the line. "Please, sir," said Vartan, "what is snow?"

Aram knew what snow was. His family had come from Anatolia, and he remembered the thin blanket of cold whiteness that often covered the ground for months at a time. The children who had come from the warmer areas of Turkey had never seen snow. Aram also knew that some of the boys had been born after the escape from Turkey; they only knew the milder weather of Greece.

When Mr. Melkonian explained about snow, some of the boys chuckled in disbelief. Then he told them more about Canada. People from all over the world came there to live in peace. There was plenty of food and land and jobs. And no war.

To live in a place without soldiers and war would be grand, thought Aram. Still, he knew he would never leave Corfu. Who would look after his grandmother? Each Sunday, his grandmother visited him at the orphanage. He would give her the bits of food that he had scrounged and collected. Sometimes that was all she had to eat. Besides, all his friends were here.

"Fifty of you will be coming back to Canada with me," said Mr. Melkonian. "Do I have any volunteers?"

"I volunteer," said Mgerdich, raising his hand.

Aram looked over at his young friend in amazement, and whispered under his breath, "put your hand down." Mikayel, Zaven, Taniel, Vartan and Sarkis also put up their hands. A few other boys put up their hands, too.

But that was not nearly enough.

Mrs. Walker's office

I won't go!" said Aram.

"There are hundreds of new orphans coming into Corfu every day, Aram," said Mrs. Walker. "When we find homes for you, you must go."

"Why don't you take one of the other boys instead of me?"

"You are the oldest, and your grandmother fears for your safety."

"I have to stay here to look after her," argued Aram. Mrs. Walker looked him in the eye. "Your grandmother is more worried about you than herself. That's why she brought you to the orphanage in the first place."

"I know that," said Aram. His memory flashed with an

image of the two of them, huddled together for warmth in a doorstep. He and his grandmother had gone days without food before she made her decision.

"I know you have been giving her food," said Mrs. Walker. "I will make sure she doesn't starve."

Aram could feel tears stinging his eyes, but he fought to hold them back.

"Why does she fear for my safety?"

"You will soon be a man," said Mrs. Walker. "And in these uncertain times, no Armenian man is safe."

Aram was silent. His father had been shot before his eyes. He remembered the last time he saw his mother. She was marching in the desert, a Turkish soldier holding a bayonet to her back. With a swirl of dust she was gone. When he found his grandmother and escaped with her to Corfu, he believed they would be safe.

"What about our teachers?" asked Aram. "Are they safe?"

Mrs. Walker didn't answer.

"I won't go," said Aram defiantly. He ran out of the room, slamming the door behind him. Then Aram ran past the barracks. He ran past groups of children who were taking their lessons. He ran past others who were playing. He ran all the way down to the sea. He took off his shirt and dove in.

Aram plunged down to the bottom with his eyes wide open, and grabbed a handful of sand. Maybe I should rub this into my eyes, he thought. If they think I have an eye infection, they won't make me go to Canada. He swam underwater for as long as he could, his hand gripped tightly around the sand. The coolness of the water cleared his mind.

Mgerdich is going, he thought. Grandmother and Mrs. Walker both want me to leave. Maybe I should. Maybe I could find enough money in the Canadian trees to buy passage for Grandmother. Aram slowly opened his hand. The sand billowed out like smoke in the water, and disappeared. He swam back to shore.

Ghost Ship

Nurse Balakian held scissors and a comb. One by one, she gave the fifty boys a very short haircut. Aram's head felt light. His neck itched from the bits of cut hair that still clung there. After the haircuts, Mrs. Walker shot a squirt of lice soap onto each scalp, and then sent each boy to the dormitory.

A giant tub of hot water was waiting. Aram jumped in, glad to have a bath in water that had only been used a few times. He massaged his head with the smelly soap, and then dunked it under the water to rinse out the suds. He scrambled out of the tub before Vartan jumped in.

After he dried himself, Aram sorted through a pile of fresh clothing—shirts with

buttons, and shorts to match—and found two sets that fit. Next to the clothing was a pile of sandals. If they were going to Canada, wouldn't they need boots?

"It is cold for only part of the year," explained Mrs. Walker.

Maybe it won't be so different from home after all, thought Aram hopefully.

When they were all clean and dressed, Mrs. Walker pulled from her pocket a pouch that jangled with coins. She gave each boy one of the small coins. Aram looked at his. It was silver colored and had the profile of a king's face on one side and a wreath on the other. He bit it, and it felt satisfyingly solid.

"It is a Canadian quarter," explained Mrs. Walker.

THAT NIGHT, after supper, Aram heard a rustle at the door. There stood his grandmother. Before she could say a word, he flew into her arms.

"I can't leave you," he said, hugging her tight.

"You must," she said. "When you get to Canada, you will write to me."

"But where would I send the letter?" asked Aram, swallowing his sadness.

"Send it to Mrs. Walker," replied his grandmother. "She will find me."

That night, Aram tried to sleep. He tossed and turned on his mattress on the floor. When Mr. Chechian stepped

into the room with a lantern in his hand, Aram sat up like a shot.

"Is something wrong?"

"Shhh," said Mr. Chechian. "Follow me," he whispered. "Bring Mgerdich with you. Don't wake the others."

Mgerdich and Aram slipped outside. Mr. Chechian gathered up Zaven, Mikayel, Taniel, Vartan, and Sarkis—all the boys who were leaving the next morning.

"He looks so sad," Aram whispered to Mgerdich.

"I think he's going to miss us," said Mgerdich.

"Also," said Aram, "it is not safe for him to stay here."

Mr. Chechian clapped his hands lightly to get their attention. "I have prepared a treat for you," he said. "Follow me."

He held the lantern up high. The boys, in sleepy clusters, followed.

They hiked through the woods, which opened up onto a hill overlooking the sea.

"We're here," said Mr. Chechian, pointing.

Aram looked down and gasped in wonder.

Lanterns had been dropped onto the surface of the water. They bobbed and sparkled like jewels. Aram blinked. There was something else down there. He looked up at Mr. Chechian.

"It is a goodbye secret just for you," said Mr. Chechian.

What would Mrs. Walker think?

Mikayel was the first to jump in. Then, one by one, Vartan, Zaven, Taniel, Mgerdich, Aram, and the other boys peeled off their nightshirts and dove in after him.

As Aram swam deeper, his eyes widened with awe. Just beneath them was the skeleton of a huge sunken sailboat. It was very old—and three-masted. Aram swam under the beams. He swam around one mast, marveling at the ghostly beauty.

He would never forget the sight as long as he lived.

June 11, 1923

Aram, Box 8

Aram didn't think he'd be able to rest after he and the other boys hiked back from their swim. But as soon as his head hit the mattress, he was sound asleep.

The next morning, he rolled up his mattress for the last time. He leaned it against the wall with all the others. His stomach fluttered with excitement and dread. Mrs. Walker had given each boy a wooden box with a number on it, and his was box eight. He packed his second set of clothing and his coin. Mrs. Walker had found him a pencil, some paper, and envelopes. He packed those, too.

Then Aram left the dormitory for the last time.

He was far too excited to eat even a bite of bread, but

he gulped down his mug of sweetened tea.

Mrs. Walker blew her whistle. "Line up according to the number on your box, please."

Aram and Mgerdich carried their boxes to Mrs. Walker.

"My box is nine," said Mgerdich.

"You're right behind me, then," said Aram.

Mrs. Walker led the first group of boys down to the dock.

"Look at how small it is," said Aram, pointing to a skiff that was tied to the pier.

"This isn't the boat that will take us to Canada, is it?" asked Mgerdich, his eyes round with fear.

"Look out there," said Aram, squinting and pointing out to sea. A cargo ship was waiting in the distance.

"Oh, good," said Mgerdich.

As they waited at the dock, Aram's grandmother arrived. Her eyes were red from crying, but she had a brave smile on her lips.

"This is the right choice," she said, hugging him tight.

Aram hugged her back. He never wanted to let her go. He knew she was worried about him, though. He didn't want that.

"I will be fine," Aram said, in his bravest voice. He gave her one last hug.

His grandmother looked so sad that he almost began to cry.

"Take this," she said. She shoved a piece of cloth into his hands, then turned and walked away.

"Grandmother!" he called. She did not turn back.

He opened his hands. It was a tattered sunset-colored veil that had belonged to his mother. Aram held it to his face. He breathed in the faint scent of apricot blossoms.

Mrs. Walker came over to Aram and gently took his arm. "It is time," she said. They walked to the edge of the dock together. "Up you get," said Mrs. Walker, helping Aram. Then she helped Taniel and the other boys across the wooden ramp and into the boat. Aram clutched the side of the little boat. It bobbed up and down as each boy got in. When all the seats were taken, the boatman pushed off.

Aram looked down into the water from the side of the boat. Its crisp blueness reminded him of their swim the night before. He thought of the ghostly skeleton ship.

Would they arrive safely in Canada, or would their ship sink, too? Maybe it was safer to stay in Corfu, after all.

Before he knew it, the little boat had bumped up against the side of the cargo ship. Two strong arms grabbed Aram and lifted him up. When all the boys were on the ship, the little boat went back for more.

Mgerdich and Aram leaned against the railing of the deck and looked back to shore. Aram could see a cluster of women standing by the dock. There was Taniel's sister. She looked so small and sad, waving her arms with all her might. Beside her was Aram's grandmother. He waved the veil. She took off her own black veil and waved back.

Aram gulped in sorrow. "I have to go back," he cried.

Mgerdich grabbed his arm. "Stay with me, please." Aram looked in the boy's eyes and saw tears. He turned back and watched as his grandmother slowly walked away.

Mr. Melkonian, the man from Canada, was supposed to be their chaperone. But even after all the boys were on the big ship, Mr. Melkonian was nowhere to be seen. The boys leaned against the railing, the sun hot on their heads.

The ship waited and waited and waited. Then there was a hum of activity on shore. A man with a suitcase jumped into the boat and was ferried over to the ship. Aram gasped in surprise. It was Mr. Chechian.

"Boys," he said, grinning broadly. "Mr. Melkonian is too ill to travel. I will accompany you to Canada."

The ship headed out to open sea.

ARAM SPENT MOST of the first day leaning over the side of the ship and throwing up.

Mgerdich wasn't sick at all. That afternoon, Aram saw Mikayel hoist Mgerdich on his shoulders as they both leaned over the side of the ship.

"Do you want to fall overboard and drown?" shouted Aram. He grabbed the younger boy by the waist, and pulled him down to safety.

"I was holding on tightly," said Mgerdich.

Aram sighed. He would have to watch Mgerdich more carefully from now on.

On the second day, Aram looked down at the water. Just above the surface was a school of flying fish, shimmering like silver darts.

The ship docked briefly at an island on the third day. Aram watched dark-skinned men diving into the sea. They were searching for coins, which rich tourists had tossed into the water from other ships.

After five days, the ship docked at Marseilles.

"Can you hear that?" asked Mgerdich, cupping a hand to his ear.

Aram did the same. "They're speaking Armenian."

"What are they all doing in France?" asked Mgerdich.

"Maybe they're escaping, just like us."

The two boys stared at the crowd. They saw grandmothers and children, most wearing rags.

"Where are the fathers and older brothers?" asked Mgerdich.

"Where are the mothers and older sisters?" wondered Aram.

Just then, Mr. Chechian stepped between the two boys. He put one hand on Aram's shoulder and another on Mgerdich's.

"So many Armenians were killed simply because they weren't Turkish."

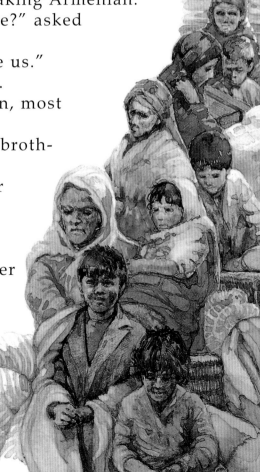

Mgerdich looked confused, but Aram knew what Mr. Chechian was talking about. The government declared that Turkey was for Turks.

"But those grandmothers and children aren't Turkish either," said Mgerdich.

"The very young and the very old are not considered as much of a threat," explained Mr. Chechian.

Just then Aram noticed a blue-eyed man on the docks. He wore a brown tweed suit, and his face was red from the heat. He mopped his brow with a handkerchief.

"Come, boys! Come!" The man said in Armenian. "I am Mr. Braxton, a missionary from the Lord Mayor's Fund in Britain. One night in Marseilles, and then you board the train to Paris."

The boys lined up according to the number on their boxes. Aram was glad to walk down the gangplank and onto solid ground. He could feel himself swaying back and forth as if he were still on the ship. Mgerdich had no such problem. He ran down the gangplank, clutching his wooden box to his chest.

That evening, Mr. Braxton took them all to a restaurant. He spoke to the waiter in French. Moments later, golden buns, fresh from the oven, were set on each table. The boys devoured them in an instant. When the waiter came out half an hour later with a platter of whole chickens, Aram gasped in disbelief. Meat.

"Eat, boys," said Mr. Braxton with a grin. "We've got a long trip ahead of us."

June 19, 1923

Disaster!

I want to sit right here!" exclaimed Mgerdich, as he plopped himself down in a seat by the window. Aram followed his friend into the train compartment. He looked around in awe. He had never seen anything quite like it.

His mind flashed back to the days after his parents had been killed, when he and his grandmother fled Turkey. There were so many orphans and so few Armenian adults left alive. How would they escape? Aram was too little to take such a long journey on foot, so his grandmother used her last coins to buy a donkey. Aram was put in one wicker basket, and another child was put in a second basket.

Then the baskets were strapped together and hoisted across the donkey's back. A third child sat in the middle— right on the donkey's back. Aram could still remember looking out through the holes in the wicker. He could see his grandmother walking beside him. His grandmother's quick thinking had saved not only his life but the lives of two other children.

What would his grandmother think of this train? It was so fancy, with high-backed chairs facing each other, and a sliding wooden door with a glass window that closed. The whole compartment was like a private little room. The best part of all was the huge glass window, which looked out onto the station platform.

Mgerdich kneeled on one of the chairs and balanced on the window, his nose pressed flat against the glass. "I'm going to see everything!"

Sarkis, Mikayel, Taniel, Vartan, and Zaven climbed onto the train, too. So did Mr. Chechian and the other boys. There was so much room that Aram and Mgerdich were in a compartment all to themselves. As the train left the station, both boys stared out the window. The city changed to fields and meadows. Aram took out the paper and pencil from his box. He began a letter to his grandmother.

By midday, Aram was dizzy from watching cows and orchards speed past. He closed his eyes and imagined that he was back in the wicker basket. The train's rhythmic movement lulled him to sleep.

He woke up with a start. It was hot. The sun beat through the glass window. Mgerdich had taken off his shirt and sandals. He had cranked the window open a little bit. Air came through the top, but there wasn't much of a breeze. Mgerdich leaned against the window and stuck his hands out to cool them. The door to the compartment slid open, and Mr. Chechian stepped in.

"This is for you," he said. He set down an orange and some bread for each of them. "They will be coming around with hot tea shortly." He looked at Mgerdich and frowned. "Keep your hands inside."

Mgerdich pulled his hands in. He sat down in his chair. Mr. Chechian left the compartment. As soon as he was gone, Mgerdich scrambled back up to the window. He cranked it completely open. He sat right on the frame, with his hands on his lap.

"See?" he said, grinning. "My hands are inside."

Aram stood up and tried to grab Mgerdich by his feet, but the boy kicked him away.

"Sit down," said Aram angrily.

"I am sitting."

Aram grabbed the boy by the waist. Mgerdich squirmed away from his grasp. Then, as Aram watched in horror, the boy tumbled out of the window. Aram lunged and tried to grab him. It was too late.

He was gone.

"Mgerdich!" Aram called out the open window. For just a second, he saw the crumpled heap of his friend amidst a cluster of bushes. Then the sight was gone.

Aram flung open the door to the compartment. He ran down the aisle, screaming, "Stop the train! Stop the train! Mgerdich fell out the window!"

Mr. Chechian burst out of the next compartment. He threw down his bags of food and pulled, hard, on the emergency cord.

The train stopped with such force that Aram fell forward on to his face. A dozen sliding doors opened at once. Children tumbled out into the aisle, screaming.

Mr. Chechian ran to the exit. He threw open the door. He jumped to the ground and ran. Aram followed, with Mikayel close behind.

They found Mgerdich by some thorny bushes. He was sprawled on his back and moaning with pain. Blood trickled down the side of his face. One of his eyes was already swollen shut. His legs and chest were covered in scratches. To Aram's relief, he was alive.

Mr. Chechian bent down beside the boy. "Where does it hurt?" he asked.

"My face!" cried Mgerdich.

Mr. Chechian pulled a handkerchief from his pocket. He gently dabbed at the blood. A deep scratch went from under Mgerdich's hair down to his chin. Mr. Chechian gingerly lifted the swollen eyelid. "Can you see me?" he asked.

"Yes," said Mgerdich.

"Thank goodness," said Mr. Chechian. Then he turned and pointed to Aram and Mikayel. "Get two long, straight branches—and a blanket from the train," he said. "We need to make a stretcher."

CHAPTER 6

June 21, 1923

Hospital

The train pulled into Paris. Aram watched with a worried frown as Mr. Braxton helped an ambulance worker carry Mgerdich on his makeshift stretcher onto the platform.

"Where are they taking him?" he asked Mr. Chechian.

"To the hospital," Mr. Chechian replied. "He'll be fine."

Mr. Chechian clapped his hands to get all the boys' attention. "Line up here, please." Then he and Mr. Braxton divided them into groups, according to their numbers.

"Group one, come with me," said Mr. Chechian. Aram followed, feeling sad that Mgerdich was no longer right behind him.

Mr. Chechian lined the boys up in front of a curtained-off area in the train station. One by one, they entered. Aram stepped in. He was greeted by two men in white coats.

"Take off your clothing," said one. "Sit up here." The man pointed to an examining table covered in a white sheet. Aram did as he was told. He waited patiently as one shone a light into his eyes, while the other poked at his ears and examined every inch of his scalp and skin.

"You pass," said one of the men.

Sarkis and two other boys didn't pass. They had eye infections. The missionary hired a car that took them to the hospital, too. Aram wasn't too upset about this. "At least Mgerdich won't be all alone."

Mr. Braxton and Mr. Chechian had the boys line up. Aram held his box to his chest and turned to say something to Mgerdich, before reminding himself again that Mgerdich wasn't there. Aram took a deep breath and blinked back tears. He hoped Mgerdich would heal quickly.

Mr. Chechian clapped his hands and the boys climbed onto the train. Aram chose a place to sit all by himself. He had so much to think about. The train took them on a short trip from Paris to Cherbourg. Their ship was waiting. They were given a quick dinner on shore, and then they boarded the ship that night.

CHAPTER 7

June 21, 1923

On the SS *Minnedosa*

I want one of the beds hanging from the ceiling," said Mikayel. He had just stepped into the stateroom. He had his wooden box under one arm and was peering over the heads of Taniel and Zaven.

"I'd like to sleep on the bottom," said Zaven. His eyes were round with concern as he stared at the upper beds.

"Me too," said Taniel.

With a grin, Mikayel tossed his box onto one of the upper beds. He hoisted himself up. "Let's just hope the ocean isn't too rocky or I'll have a long way to fall."

Aram scrambled up and stretched out on the other upper bed. The bunk was so close to the ceiling that when he reached up, he could touch it. The mattress was soft, though. As long as he didn't need to vomit, it would be fine.

"Let's explore," Aram said. He hopped down and darted out the doorway. The other boys followed. They ran down the corridor toward the stairs.

SMACK.

Aram ran into an old man in a suit, knocking him right down. The man said something to him in what was probably English, but Aram didn't understand. There was no mistaking the look on the man's face, however. Aram extended his hand to help the man to his feet. The man just shook his fist and kept on yelling.

"Let's get out of here," said Mikayel.

The boys ran up the stairs.

The steamship SS *Minnedosa* was a far cry from the cargo ship the boys had taken from Corfu to Marseilles. That one had been old, and it smelled bad. Everyone on the cargo ship had been an orphan or a refugee. Here, there were people who didn't speak a word of Armenian, Turkish, or Greek. They were dressed in store-bought clothing and smelled like flowers. The SS *Minnedosa* was a palace on water, complete with a huge dining room. And a swimming pool.

"Too bad it doesn't have water in it," said Mikayel.

The dining room was on the main deck, toward the front of the ship. Aram pushed open the door and the boys stepped in. They were amazed by the sight. The room was filled with fancy chairs pulled up to round tables covered with crisp white tablecloths. Each table was set with knives and forks and sparkling glasses. Aram's heart pounded in his chest. It would be scary to eat here with all these rich people, but the food was probably tasty.

"The dining room is closed until 8:00 p.m.," said a woman's voice behind them. "That's another two hours."

Aram turned around. It was a woman with a white

apron over a blue dress, her hair tied in a bun. She stood with her arms crossed over her chest.

"You speak Armenian?" said Aram.

"I am Armenian," said the woman.

"I am Aram, and these are my friends, Mikayel, Taniel, and Zaven."

"I am Anoush, but people here call me Annie," said the woman. "You must be on your best behavior," she added sternly. "I don't want you to give Armenians a bad name."

"We will be good," said Aram solemnly. The other boys just giggled and ran away.

Before dinner that night, Mr. Chechian made sure that

all the boys washed their hands and faces. They all put on their second set of clothing. As Mr. Chechian led them into the dining room, conversation stopped. Aram could feel a hundred pair of eyes look them up and down. Even with a scrubbed face and dressed in clean clothes, Aram could feel his cheeks burn with embarrassment. The women wore long pastel-colored dresses and necklaces and earrings. The men wore dark suits. No one else wore sandals. Once the boys settled into their places, the other diners looked away and continued with their conversations.

Annie served the first course: a bowl of green soup.

At the orphanage, Aram had become used to lining up with the rest of the boys for food. He would scoop up bits of stewed vegetables with a slice of bread or a layer of onion. When he and his grandmother had begged in the streets, the food they shared was eaten on the spot. Even in the restaurant in Paris, the boys had used their hands.

Aram looked down at the bowl of green soup. He was about to take the bowl in his hands when Mr. Chechian coughed loudly. Aram looked up at his teacher, who picked up a spoon from beside his bowl and stared at the boys meaningfully.

One by one, the boys picked up their spoons, too. They watched as Mr. Chechian scooped up a spoonful of soup and held it to his lips. They did the same. Then, with a loud noise, Mr. Chechian slurped every last speck of soup off his spoon. In unison, the boys did the same.

Conversation stopped. A hundred pair of eyes turned in disapproval.

Annie rushed over to the table. In a loud whisper, she said in Armenian, "Use the spoons but don't make the noise!"

Mr. Chechian turned bright red. "Sorry," he said.

The boys enjoyed the good weather while it lasted. Mr. Chechian assembled them all on the promenade deck, and they marched around the entire ship, singing the Armenian national anthem. As they marched, Aram looked out toward France. He worried about Mgerdich.

Each day, the boys enjoyed lots of food and plenty of fresh air. Once, Mr. Chechian took them below-decks to watch the engines. Another time, one of the stewards found a ball, and some of the boys played soccer on the deck. When the weather turned chilly, Aram and his friends went back to their rooms to play.

Aram woke up early on the third morning with a horrible feeling in his stomach. He jumped down from his bed and stepped out into the hallway. He could feel the ship sway so deeply from side to side that he had to hold onto the railing to keep his balance. He climbed the stairs and stepped onto the deck. The sun was just barely peeking over the horizon. He breathed in deeply and realized that the air smelled different. Before, there had always been a whiff of the land—of something rotting, but now the air was crisp and clean. The water was a now deeper shade of blue.

As Aram walked back down the stairs, he nearly stumbled. The ship pitched and rolled. He ran down the hall to the bathroom and threw up.

For more than two days, the ship tumbled and rocked on the rolling sea. Aram was sick most of the time. Whenever he felt a bit better, he went up to the top deck and peered beyond the railing. No matter what direction he looked in, he could see no land. It was a little scary, but the cool sea air washed over his face and calmed him. He thought about his grandmother and closed his eyes. The rollicking sea felt like the lope of the donkey that had carried him in the wicker basket to safety. At night, he dreamed of Canada: a land where gold was so plentiful it grew on trees. He would pluck that gold and buy his grandmother's safety. He could hardly wait.

THE MANY DAYS of seasickness blended all together for Aram, but the first day he saw land was special. First, it was just a glimmer on the horizon, but then he could make out rocks and trees.

"I see buildings," said Aram.

The boys gathered round and watched as their ship entered the St. Lawrence River. They passed clusters of houses and small communities, but the ship didn't stop.

CHAPTER 8

Late afternoon, June 29, 1923

Port of Quebec

We're coming into port!" shouted Aram.

Mikayel and the other boys looked out where Aram pointed. They cheered.

The boys scampered below to pack up their belongings, then clutched their wooden boxes and waited as the *SS Minnedosa* pulled into the dock.

A group of men and women in modern suits and hats waited at the dock to greet them. One man walked forward as they stepped onto land. He said something to them in English.

Mr. Chechian translated. "This is Dr. Vining," he said. "He is with the Armenian Relief Fund of Canada."

Aram grinned and bowed. The other boys did the same. A few people from the group handed each of the boys a book. Aram opened his and was filled with gratitude. It was a Bible, written in English but also in Armenian.

Dr. Vining motioned with his hand for them all to follow him. As they walked toward a large brick building, Aram saw some trees with leaves unlike any he had seen before. There were glimmers of yellow amidst the green five-pointed leaves.

"It's gold!" said Aram, grinning to Mikayel. It would take Aram no time at all to pick enough gold to pay for his grandmother's passage to Canada. He could hardly wait to see her.

The two boys set down their boxes and ran to the trees. Dr. Vining stood by, watching silently with a confused smile on his face. Aram grabbed a handful of yellow. He was surprised by how light it was. Even his Canadian quarter felt more solid than this! He held the yellow to his nose and sniffed. It smelled like a flower. Does gold smell like flowers? He wondered. He rubbed it between his fingers. The tiny cluster of petals fell apart.

"It's only a flower," he said with disappointment.

"That's a sugar maple tree," said Dr. Vining. Then he explained something to Mr. Chechian.

"These are not trees of gold," explained Mr. Chechian. "But in the summer, the sap from these trees is like liquid sugar."

"Gold would have been better," whispered Aram under his breath as he and Mikayel walked with the others into the building.

Inside, a very fat woman stood behind a table that held giant bowls of fruit. The sight reminded Aram of the days when he and his grandmother lived on the street. They would go to the market because sometimes they could find squished fruit on the ground. These Canadian fruits were strange looking. There were no kumquats, figs, apricots, or prickly pears. Even the fruits that Aram recognized looked different. The apples were redder, the strawberries and cherries were bigger, and the grapes were paler. Taniel asked for some strawberries and Vartan wanted some cherries. Mikayel asked for an apple. When it was Aram's turn, the familiar fruit was running out, so the woman handed him something long and yellow. He held it to his nose and sniffed. The scent reminded him of figs. He tried to bite it, but it was tough and bitter. He asked the woman in Armenian, "What is this?"

"Banana," she said, smiling.

Was he holding a banana, or did "banana" mean "move on" in English? Aram wasn't sure.

Dr. Vining came over. "Banana," he said. The woman gave him one, too. Aram watched as Dr. Vining peeled it and took a bite. Aram did the same. It was delicious!

Aram walked over to the table and sat down with the other boys. Aram watched Mikayel eat the last of his apple.

As always, he popped the whole core—seeds and all—into his mouth. He chewed and swallowed. Then he smacked his lips with satisfaction.

Some of the Canadians were sitting at another table. Aram elbowed Mikayel. "Look," he said. The boys watched a woman eat an apple. She took tiny bites, and then chewed with a bored look on her face. When there was nothing left but the core, seeds, and stem, she got up and tossed it in the garbage.

"Why didn't she eat it?" asked Mikayel in amazement.

Aram couldn't imagine wasting food like that. He wished he could pack up some Canadian fruit and mail it to his grandmother.

"Does that taste good?" Mikayel asked Aram, pointing at the last of his banana.

"Try it," said Aram. "It's sweet." He broke off a bit and handed it to his friend.

As Aram chewed the remains of his banana, he watched as Mr. Chechian went over to talk to Dr. Vining. It looked like the two men were arguing. Dr. Vining walked away.

Aram nudged Mikayel. "Something is wrong."

The two boys got up and walked over. "Excuse me, sir," said Aram. "Is something the matter?"

Mr. Chechian looked down. Aram was startled by the deep sadness in the man's eyes.

"Please don't worry about me," Mr. Chechian said.

As the two boys walked away, Aram whispered to his friend, "But I am worried."

Just as they had in Paris, the boys lined up and were checked over by doctors. Then they received new clothing. Aram had expected real shoes and fine suits like he had seen the Canadian men wearing. But he was wrong.

"This looks just like what we already have," he said to Mikayel in surprise.

"But these are clean," said Mikayel.

They didn't get shoes or socks at all, so they kept their old sandals.

Then they were whisked away to another train. It was different from the one in France. The inside of the car was one big compartment, with an aisle down the middle and seats on either side.

Mikayel stood on one of the seats, reached up, and pulled down on a handle. "Look at this," he said. "A bed!"

The train started moving. A man in a uniform opened the door at the end of the compartment and stepped in. He had a grin on his face. He gave each boy a small rectangle of something wrapped in paper. Aram sniffed his. It smelled like mint. The man took one of the rectangles and peeled the paper off. He popped the rectangle into his mouth and chewed.

"Spearmint gum!" he said.

Aram didn't know what the man was saying, but the

boy could tell that
they had received a treat. He popped the gum
in his mouth and marveled at the explosion of flavor
as he chewed.

That night, some of the boys slept in the pull-out beds.
Aram fell asleep curled up on one of the seats. His
wooden box rested beside him.

CHAPTER 9

June 30, 1923

Montreal

Whard already stopped. The boys were led off the train and on to another. Then women in black dresses and hats stepped on to the train. They carried trays of tall glasses filled with something white. Aram picked up one of the glasses. He took a long gulp, then nearly choked in surprise. He had been expecting a mouthful of *tan*—a soured milk drink popular in Greece and Turkey. Instead of the familiar yogurt-like taste, his mouth was filled with a sweet creaminess. Fresh milk! The taste was familiar from long, long ago. It was delicious.

Another lady held out a basket of small, round, bread-

looking things, with something pale yellow smeared on top.

"Biscuit," she said. She handed him one.

Aram smiled and examined it carefully. He was used to flat bread, not this round, puffy stuff. He sniffed it. Mmmm! He took a bite. It was crumbly, salty, and delicious! What Aram loved the most was the creamy richness of the yellow topping. He pointed to it and looked at the lady."

"That is butter," she said.

Aram wished his grandmother was there to share. He was sure she had never tasted anything like it in her life.

When they were finished, Aram saw Mr. Chechian step off the train and sit down on the edge of one of the benches on the platform. He had a sad look on his face.

Aram pushed open the door and stepped outside. He walked over to Mr. Chechian.

"Please, sir, tell me what is wrong."

Mr. Chechian looked up. He didn't say anything for a long time. Finally, he spoke quietly. "Dr. Vining is sending me back to Corfu as soon as we get to the Georgetown farm."

"Why would he do that?" asked Aram, alarmed.

"Dr. Vining says it can't be helped." Mr. Chechian put his head in his hands.

"Surely he knows what will happen to you if you go back?" An image of Turkish soldiers with bayonets flashed in Aram's mind. The soldiers weren't bothering the children and women anymore, but Armenian men were not safe.

"He says the government will not allow me to become a Canadian."

"Why not?" asked Aram.

"Because I am an adult. The immigration authorities have reached their quota of Armenian men."

Aram could feel his face get hot. His beloved teacher was one of the few Armenian men who had escaped from Turkey. He was like the father that Aram had lost. He could feel a deep anger building within him. Aram had lost his father and his mother. He had lost his brother, and now he was far away from his grandmother and Mgerdich. He would not let anyone hurt Mr. Chechian!

"We'll see about that," said Aram. Then he turned and walked away.

Aram grabbed his wooden box from the seat and then looked around. He needed a place to sit by himself so he

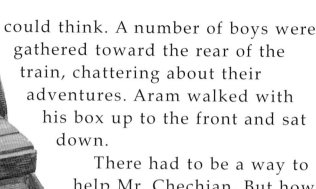

could think. A number of boys were gathered toward the rear of the train, chattering about their adventures. Aram walked with his box up to the front and sat down.

There had to be a way to help Mr. Chechian. But how? He opened his wooden box and pulled out the letter that he had written to his grandmother. He tried to read it, but his eyes were blurred with tears of anger.

Everything he had hoped for was falling apart. Mgerdich was in the hospital in France—would he ever get to Canada? Aram hadn't found gold in the trees yet, so he still couldn't save his grandmother. And now his beloved teacher was about to be sent back.

Aram squeezed his eyes tight. One big teardrop rolled off his cheek and plopped into his box. He looked down. The tear had landed on his coin. Aram picked up the quarter and dried it off. He felt the weight of it in his hand. It wasn't gold, but surely it could buy more than stamps. He wanted to mail the letter to his grandmother, but perhaps someone else needed the money more. It was a difficult choice.

Aram put the quarter in his pocket and hurried to the back of the train. "All of you," he said. "We need to talk." The boys looked up. "They're sending Mr. Chechian back to Corfu," he said.

The boys were stunned.

Finally, Mikayel said, "What can we do to change Dr. Vining's mind?"

"I was thinking about it," said Aram. "What if we collected our money and gave it to Dr. Vining? Maybe we could buy Mr. Chechian's way to Canada."

"I would give up my quarter for Mr. Chechian," said Vartan right away. He reached into his pocket and handed Aram his coin.

"I would give my quarter, too," said Taniel, "but I want to mail my letter." Tears welled up in the little boy's eyes. "My sister is still in Corfu. She'll worry if she doesn't hear from me."

Aram thought of his own letter. He thought of his grandmother, too. He knew exactly how Taniel felt. "Let's forget about the letters right now," said Aram. "Mr. Chechian's life is more important."

Taniel took a deep breath. "Okay," he said in a small voice. Then he reached into his pocket and dug out his coin.

CHAPTER 10

Orphan's Gold

One by one, the boys handed their quarters to Aram. There were so many that Aram couldn't hold them all. Mikayel rooted through his own wooden box. "Put them in this," he said, holding out his extra shirt.

Aram poured the coins into the shirt, then tied it into a bundle.

"One problem," said Mikayel.

"What's that?" asked Aram.

"How are we going to explain to Dr. Vining what we want to do? None of us speak English," said Mikayel.

"There is only one thing we can do," said Taniel. "We have to tell Mr. Chechian our plans."

Aram stepped off the train, hugging the precious bundle of quarters to his chest. The rest of the boys followed right behind. They walked up to their teacher.

Mr. Chechian's mind was somewhere else. He didn't even notice the boys approach.

"Sir?" said Aram.

Mr. Chechian blinked. He turned and looked at Aram. Then he noticed all the other boys crowded round.

"What is the matter?" asked Mr. Chechian.

"We have a question," said Aram. "Would money convince Dr. Vining to let you stay?"

Mr. Chechian looked from Aram's eyes to the bundle he held. "What is that?" he asked.

"Our coins," said Aram. "We have forty-six Canadian quarters. Surely Dr. Vining will let you stay if we give him our money?"

Mr. Chechian's eyes filled with tears. He opened his mouth but no words came out. He took a deep breath. "Boys, I am touched by your generosity. But even if it could help, I would not take your money."

"What do you mean, 'if it could help'?" asked Vartan.

"Dr. Vining is obeying the law," said Mr. Chechian. "I know he would let me stay if he could. After all, he arranged to bring all of you to Canada. He is a good man."

Aram knew that what his teacher said was true. But still, there had to be a way. "What if you talked to the government?" suggested Aram.

"What?" asked Mr. Chechian, alarmed.

"Take our money," said Aram. "And travel to the person in charge. If you tell him what will happen to you if you go back, he must change his mind."

"Good idea," said Mikayel. The other boys nodded in approval.

"I cannot take your money," said Mr. Chechian, again. "That would be stealing."

"We choose to give this money to you," said Aram.

"But your grandmother," said Mr. Chechian. "She needs to hear from you. You need that money for stamps." Mr. Chechian looked at the other children in the crowd. "Taniel, your sister is worried. Mikayel, Mrs. Walker is waiting to hear from you."

Aram knew from the look on Mr. Chechian's face that he wasn't in the mood for arguing. If only there was a way for the letters to be mailed and for Mr. Chechian to be safe.

Taniel stepped forward. "I have an idea," he said. He held out a packet of envelopes. "What if you mailed these letters in a single big envelope to Mrs. Walker?"

Mr. Chechian regarded Taniel with respect. "One big envelope would cost less to mail than forty-six little ones."

"Then would there be enough money left over for you?" asked Taniel in a small voice.

Mr. Chechian thought for a moment. "There should be several dollars left after I mail your letters," he said. "The person I need to see is in Ottawa. I might have enough money left over for train fare."

"But what if you don't?" asked Aram.

"Then I shall walk all the way there," said Mr. Chechian firmly.

Aram grinned with relief.

Mr. Chechian reached out and took the letters from Taniel. Aram handed him the bundle of coins.

"I will never forget your kindness," said Mr. Chechian, "And I promise that I will mail your letters."

Gone!

O ne by one the boys climbed back on the train. As it pulled out of the station, they waved. Mr. Chechian stood on the platform, hugging the bundle of coins and the packet of letters to his chest. His face was still pale, but the worried frown had been replaced by a look of determination.

Aram settled into one of the comfortable seats and set his box on his lap. He opened it and drew out his mother's sunset-colored veil. He held it to his face, breathing in the familiar scent of apricot. Aram knew that if his mother had lived, she would be proud of him right now.

He fell asleep and dreamed that his grandmother was reading his letter. He saw tears in her eyes, but they were tears of joy. She knew he was safe.

Aram hugged his wooden box in his sleep and then dreamt of Mgerdich. The boy had a healed scar like a railway track down the side his face. He was happy and grinning as he ran from room to room at the hospital, making the other patients laugh.

Dr. Vining gently shook Aram's shoulder. He woke up with a start and rubbed the sleep out of his eyes. The train had been moving for hours. Dr. Vining asked him something, but Aram didn't know what. All he could understand was "Mr. Chechian."

"He's safe," said Aram in Armenian.

Dr. Vining frowned. He didn't understand. He threw up his hands in frustration and walked away.

Before Aram had fallen asleep, he had felt alone. Now he was glad that he and the boys had done the right thing. He missed his grandmother, but he knew Mrs. Walker would look after her. He missed Mgerdich, but he had a feeling his friend would come to Canada soon. He missed Mr. Chechian, too. He knew that he might never see his dear teacher again. The thought made him sad, but it also made him proud. Mr. Chechian would live.

A little while later, the train stopped. Dr. Vining directed the boys off the train.

"Toronto," said Dr. Vining.

Aram didn't know what he meant by that, but he smiled and nodded. Maybe "Toronto" was a tasty treat?

They were taken to a wooden building where they waited until another strange kind of train appeared. Aram was amazed at how many different kinds of trains he had seen in the last few weeks. This one was part of a "radial railway." It was on tracks just like other trains, but it was electric. A line of wire ran about twelve feet above the track and it was attached to the train with another wire.

Dr. Vining stood beside the door and helped each boy step in.

CHAPTER 12

Dominion Day, July 1 1923

Georgetown Boys' Farm

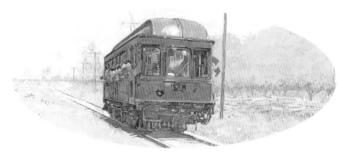

An hour later, the train stopped.

"We're here at last," said Dr. Vining.

The boys looked at him blankly.

"Home," he said.

Home? Aram knew that word. It meant being safe. Was he finally some place where the Turks wouldn't find him? Was his journey finally over?

Aram and the boys followed Dr. Vining. They stepped out onto a small wooden platform. Then they walked down the steps onto a narrow dirt road with tall grass growing on either side. Aram could see fields in the distance, and fences. He didn't see home.

Aram and the others followed Dr. Vining down a small laneway. Aram admired the orchards and lush green fields of grain.

"Look!" said Aram, pointing at a tree.

"It's like the one we saw when we first came to Canada," said Mikayel.

Aram remembered. It was called a maple tree, and he had thought gold grew on its branches.

Dr. Vining said something, and then motioned with his hands. Aram and the others continued to follow him. Then Dr. Vining disappeared.

Aram ran ahead to see what had happened. Dr. Vining was still there, but he had walked down a steep slope. He grinned and gestured for the boys to follow him. Some slid down and some ran, holding their boxes over their heads.

All of a sudden, the trees opened up and Aram gasped at the sight before him.

"Home," said Dr. Vining.

It was paradise. There was a rippling creek, apple orchards, and fields of wheat. There was also a long stucco building that looked freshly built.

"This is all for us?" asked Aram in amazement.

Dr. Vining didn't know the words, but he understood the sentiment. He nodded and grinned.

A group of cheering adults stood waiting for them, waving flags which were red with stripes of white and blue. In one corner was a crest with gold. The wind caught one of the flags, and it billowed out so that Aram could see clearly the bottom of the crest. There were three gold maple leaves.

This was orphan's gold. It was freedom. It was home.

In front of them stood a wooden table with platters stacked high with something that looked like little white triangles. A woman with yellow hair stepped forward and greeted the boys. "Mrs. Edwards," she said, pointing to herself. "Reverend Edwards," she said, pointing to the man standing beside her. Then she pointed to the triangles and said something else. The boys stood there, confused. Mrs. Edwards picked up one of the triangles and took a bite out of it, then said, "Mmmm! Sandwich. Eat."

Each boy took a sandwich and nibbled on it with hesitation. Would these Canadians think they were rude if they ate too much?

Then Mrs. Edwards gestured with her hands. "These are all for you. Eat."

The boys descended on the sandwiches like a cloud of locusts, while the smiling adults looked on.

That night Aram, Taniel and Mikayel, Vartan, Zaven, and the other boys slept in blankets under the stars. The newly built stucco building was not quite finished, but it would be soon. As Aram drifted off to sleep, he could feel the solid ground beneath him and he felt safe. He was no longer escaping in a basket, or in a ship, or on a train.

That night, he dreamed a brand new dream. It was about his choice to be a Canadian.

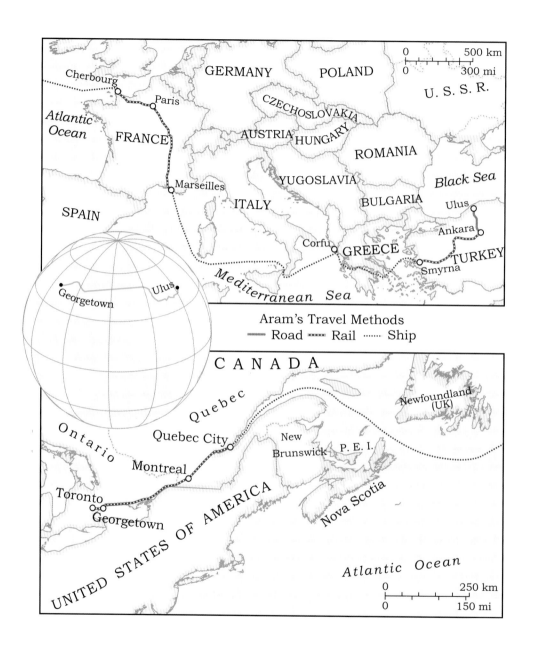

Aram's Travel Methods
— Road ▬▬▬ Rail ······ Ship

GLOSSARY

Armenian—An ancient people who populated a vast region in Asia Minor, including present-day Turkey. It is said that the Armenians can trace their ancestry to Noah. Indeed, Mount Ararat, in ancient Armenia is said to be where Noah's ark rested when the Great Flood receded. Armenians adopted Christianity in 301 AD, making them the first state to do so.

Armenian Relief Fund of Canada—An organization formed in 1922 and devoted to rescuing Armenian children whose families were killed during the Armenian genocide.

Barracks—A military building used as sleeping quarters for soldiers.

Bayonet—A knife attached to the end of a gun.

Cargo Ship—A heavy-duty ship built to carry goods rather than people.

Compartment—A small, enclosed room inside a train.

Chaperone—An adult who accompanies children and is responsible for their welfare.

Dominion Day—On October 27, 1982, July 1 officially became known as Canada Day. Before that, the day commemorating Canada's 1867 Confederation was known as Dominion Day.

Dormitory—A room or building for lots of people to sleep in.

Flag—Since before Confederation, the Red Ensign (red with the Union Jack in one corner and a crest with three maple leaves) was considered Canada's flag. With minor changes, it continued to be Canada's flag until February 15, 1965, when the current Canadian flag was adopted.

Flying Fish—A fish with large side fins that look like wings. Flying fish can jump out of the water and skim the surface.

Gangplank—A moveable ramp used to get on a boat or ship.

GLOSSARY

Immigration—The act of leaving one's home country to travel to and settle in another country.

King—In 1923, the King of Britain was George V, the father of the present Queen Elizabeth II.

Lord Mayor's Fund—A charitable group launched in Great Britain in 1915 in order to help survivors of the Armenian genocide in Turkey.

Missionary, Missionaries—A person or people who go to another country in order to give aid.

Orphanage—A home for groups of children whose parents have died.

Passage—A ticket that allows a passenger to travel, usually by sea.

Promenade Deck—The upper deck on a ship. Passengers are allowed to walk on this deck.

Quota—A set number.

Radial railway—Decades ago, people could travel from city to city in Canada by electric railway. These were referred to as "radial" because of the way the lines radiated out of a city. This form of transportation was abandoned when cars became popular.

Refugee—A person taking refuge, or shelter, in a foreign country. Refugees escape from war, persecution, or natural disasters.

Sailing ship—A wind powered ship used for traveling long distances. Vessels with three masts are referred to as ships, while those with one or two masts are referred to as boats.

Skiff—A small flat-bottomed boat. The skiff in this story is propelled with a long pole.

Sleeper—a railroad car designed with comfortable pull-down beds stored above the passenger seats. They came into use in 1894. The sleeper car that the Georgetown Boys used was taken out of storage especially for their journey.

Snow boot—Old fashioned snow boots were bulky and made of rubber or plastic. They were often fleece or fur-lined, and they were pulled on top of shoes and fastened with buckles.

Stamp—In 1923, it cost $0.10 to send a standard-sized letter (under 30 grams) from Canada to Corfu. To send 46 standard letters, it would cost $4.60. But 46 standard letters sent in one big envelope would only cost approximately $1.00.

Stateroom—A small bedroom on a ship.

Steamship—Most ocean traveling ships in 1923 used steam to propel them.

Stretcher—Cloth stretched over a frame, used to transport the injured.

Stucco—A mixture of cement, sand, and lime that is applied to the outside of buildings to insulate them.

Train—The French train and the two Canadian trains that the Georgetown Boys traveled on were steam-powered locomotives.

Turkish—The original Turks were clusters of nomadic tribes settled in the region of modern day Turkey in 800 AD. The Turkish nation adopted the Muslim religion centuries ago. Armenian and Turkish cultures lived side by side for centuries, intermarrying and trading together but keeping their own distinct cultures. Because of their long and close contact, the difference between Turks and Armenians is cultural and religious, not racial. Modern Turkey is the only middle/near eastern country that is secular—ruled by a non-religious government. Armenians and Turks have been uneasy neighbors for five centuries, with Armenia frequently being conquered by various Turkish kingdoms. The Armenian quest for religious and cultural freedom in their homeland was considered treason by various Turkish governments.

SUGGESTED READING

Children's novels about the Armenian genocide:

Kherdian, David. *The Road from Home*. New York: Greenwillow, 1995.

Skrypuch, Marsha Forchuk. *The Hunger*. Toronto: Dundurn Press, 1999.

Skrypuch, Marsha Forchuk. *Nobody's Child*. Toronto: Dundurn Press, 2004.

Internet:

Armenian National Institute: http://www.armenian-genocide.org/

The author's website: http://www.calla.com

Film:

The Georgetown Boys
Producer/Director:
Dorothy Manoukian
Canadian Filmakers Distribution Centre, 1987. DVD (26 minutes). For purchasing information, please contact: gtb@photogrphos.com or phone 514-338-3862.

The Georgetown Boys
by Isabel Kaprielian
VHS (12 minutes)
Includes teacher's guide
For purchasing information, please contact: ikaprielian@oise.utoronto.ca or phone 416-769-0843.

My Son Shall Be Armenian
Director/Researcher: Hagop Goudsouzian
National Film Board of Canada, 2005. VHS (81 minutes) with subtitles: available in original French version: *Mon fils sera arménien*. For purchasing information, please contact: www.nfb.ca or phone 514-283-9450

I N D E X

INDEX

MARSHA FORCHUK SKRYPUCH is the author of many books for children, including *Silver Threads, Enough, The Hunger*, and *Hope's War*. Her novel about the Armenian genocide, *Nobody's Child*, was nominated for the Red Maple Award, the Alberta Rocky Mountain Book Award, and the B.C. Stellar Award; it was also listed by Resource Links as a Best Book. *Aram's Choice* is based on the story of Kevork Kevorkian, one of the original Georgetown Boys—a group of Armenian orphans brought to Georgetown, Ontario, in 1923. An English scholar and former librarian, Marsha lives in Brantford, Ontario, with her husband and son.

MURIEL WOOD was born in Kent, England. She obtained her diploma in design and painting at the Canterbury College of Art before immigrating to Canada. Since the early 1960s her artwork has appeared in many places: magazines, books, stamps, porcelains, and posters. In addition, she has displayed her paintings in a number of group and one-woman shows. Her children's books include *Old Bird*, L.M. Montgomery's *Anne of Green Gables*, and Margaret Laurence's *The Olden Day's Coat*. She has also illustrated the two previous titles in the New Beginnings series, *Scared Sarah* and *Lizzie's Storm*. A former instructor at the Ontario College of Art and Design in Toronto, Muriel now draws and paints fulltime. She lives with her husband and two cats in Port Hope, Ontario.

ON APRIL 24, 1915, while almost everyone was consumed with the daily events of World War I, the first genocide of the twentieth century began. The new revolutionary "Young Turk" government wanted to get rid of anyone who wasn't Turkish. Their motto was: Turkey For the Turks. At the time, the largest minority in Turkey were the Armenians.

Under the pretext of enlistment in the Turkish army, the government rounded up and shot all the Armenian men of military age.

The government told the Armenian grandparents, women and children that they were being deported. Taking all the worldly goods they could carry, the remaining Armenians were marched into the desert. Soldiers forced them to march in giant circles until they ran out of food and water. One and a half million Armenians died.

After World War I, under the protection of the allied nations, the few children and elderly who somehow survived began to trickle back into Turkey. But in 1922, the political climate changed again and the survivors had no choice but to flee.

Despite the fact that Italy and Greece were at war, the Greeks opened their arms to the refugees. By the spring of 1923, 4,000 children, plus uncounted grandparents, had taken refuge on the island of Corfu. Orphans were housed in old army barracks, in caves, in abandoned mansions, and any other place where a spare roof could be found. Missionaries from Canada, Britain, and the United States did what they could with their limited resources. Because more refugees were pouring in every day, the missionaries were stretched to their limit. They appealed to the public for help.

The Armenian Relief Association of Canada was formed in 1922 with the goal of rescuing one hundred orphaned boys between the ages of eight and twelve and setting them up on a farm in Georgetown, Ontario. There the young refugees would be cared for, educated, and trained as farm helpers.

The government of Canada at the time did not consider Armenians to be desirable immigrants. In the 1920s, fewer than 1,300 Armenians were allowed to enter Canada. The Armenian Relief Association of Canada persisted and got their plan approved.

On July 1, 1923, the first forty-seven boys arrived at the farm in Georgetown, Ontario. A few weeks later, three more arrived. Another forty boys arrived in the fall of 1924. Others trickled in later, for a total of 110. The rescue of these Armenian orphans came to be known as "Canada's Noble Experiment." It was that country's first international humanitarian effort.